# THE
# DEAD
## DETECTIVE

*IN*

# THROW AWAY
# THE KEY

# THE
# DEAD
# DETECTIVE

## *IN*

# THROW AWAY
# THE KEY

### by Felix Bogarte™

Published 2003 by Books Noir Ltd, Glasgow

Copyright © 2003 Books Noir Ltd

Text written by Joan Love and Mhairi MacDiarmid,
based on a story by Mhairi MacDiarmid

A CIP catalogue for this book is available from the British Library

ISBN 1-904684-04-1

Printed and bound in the EU

www.booksnoir.com
www.deaddetective.com
info@deaddetective.com

# CONTENTS

# WHO'S WHO IN DEAD DETECTIVE LAND

### WHO IS CHARLIE CHRISTIAN?

12 year-old Charlie Christian is a born detective – and has been given the opportunity to prove himself. The Court Of Ghouls, who exist in a twilight zone between life and death have decreed that the Dead Detective, Hank Kane be sentenced to fight crime in Charlie's very own city of Glasgow! And, as Hank Kane cannot be trusted to solve cases honestly he has been instructed to take on someone he can train as a detective – someone like Charlie Christian.

### WHO IS ANNIE?

Ten year-old Annie, or "Ace" as her brother, Charlie, insists on calling her is the world's most reluctant detective. To say that she doesn't share her brother's love of all things detective would be putting it mildly – the whole investigative "scene" bores her senseless.

### WHO IS THE GRIM REAPER?

The Grim Reaper, or TG as he likes to be known,

really enjoys his work. He loves the perks of his job, annoying Hank, partying and fiddling his expenses.

## SO, WHO IS THE DEAD DETECTIVE?

The Dead Detective is Hank Kane, a crooked cop, killed in the line of duty in Los Angeles in the 1950s. Instead of passing straight over to the other side, however, Hank finds himself facing the Court Of Ghouls, who have decided that he'll have to pay for his habit of planting evidence on suspects. They sentence him to fighting crime, using only honest methods, until they are convinced that he's learnt his lesson. They instruct The Grim Reaper to keep an eye on Hank. It isn't that they don't totally trust Hank – it's just that they don't trust him at all!

Hank's other problem is his appearance. He's a skeleton! During daylight hours he has no flesh on his bones (well, he *is* dead!) and so has to stay out of sight. At night, however, providing he drinks some of his chemical compound, flesh returns to his bones and he looks almost normal. "Almost" because Hank died fifty years previously and has been catapulted forward in time to 2003.

# CHAPTER ONE
## THE PRISONER

THE Dead Detective, Hank Kane, searched frantically through his pockets. Nothing. The ringing grew more insistent, becoming louder. A call box in the distance caught his eye. The ringing noise was coming from there.

He tried to stand up; tried to walk towards the ringing telephone but his legs were stuck firmly in the sand. He shouldn't have come so far down onto the beach, ignoring the warnings of quicksand. Now, no matter how much he struggled, he only made matters worse.

First his thighs and now his waist were gripped by the greedy sand. He tried to shout for help but there was no one there, no one to hear his shouts. The sand sucked relentlessly, his hands and arms were being pulled under. He struggled to keep his head out of the sand and gasped to fill his lungs with air.

Hank suddenly found himself awake. His brow was beaded in sweat and he could still hear the distant ring of a telephone. But now he realised that it was his *office* telephone that was ringing. The sense of relief was instant. In his dream, he had been mere seconds away from suffocation and drowning. He drew deep breaths of oxygen as he struggled to free himself from the blankets, which were now tangled around his feet.

He made his way from his bedroom into his office and picked up the telephone. His throat was dry and sounded as if he'd swallowed a handful of gravel. He picked up the receiver and said "hello".

"Help me, please help me," said the plaintive voice at the other end.

"Hello," Hank repeated. "Who is this?"

"Help me, please, you have to help me," he heard again. Hank rubbed his eyes and tried to shake himself properly awake.

"Who are you?" he asked of the caller. "*How* can I help you?"

"I'm a prisoner," came the reply. "Help me escape, please."

Silence followed, although Hank could hear that the caller had not hung up.

Hank spoke more loudly. "Hello, are you still there?" There was still no response. Eventually, the dead sound of the dialling tone signalled that the caller had hung up.

Hank replaced the receiver, shaking his head. A crank call. Just where did these guys get off getting their kicks out of making weird 'phone calls'? He made his way into his tiny kitchen where he poured himself some cold orange juice.

The quicksand nightmare had rattled him. He'd been having more and more of these nightmares recently. He drank deeply and looked at the kitchen clock. 3:15 am. He pushed open the door of TG's bedroom and noticed the empty bed. Out at *The Cesspit* again, thought Hank wryly.

*The Cesspit* was a nightclub for ghouls, founded by the ever-enterprising TG (or 'The Grim Reaper' to give him his official title). Business was booming because no one had ever thought of a nightclub for dead folk before! So TG was now considering a franchise operation, carefully selecting sites in his favourite cities: Barcelona, Paris, and Prague, New York.

"It's a tax dodge," he once explained to Hank, "a million laughs; a place to hang out, do business - and prate!"

Hank drained his glass and went back into his bedroom, opening the window as wide as it could go. He didn't know which was worse; the never ending Glasgow rain or the humidity, which seemed to follow it.

Hank wondered about the call. Not many people called 'The Hank Kane Detective Agency'. He had thought that perhaps TG had something to do with it. It seemed to Hank that TG was often familiar with the cases he took on, before Hank himself was. OK, so the Grim Reaper is *expected* to be one step ahead of the game but Hank was almost convinced that TG had some way of screening the calls.

It seemed like the only cases that Hank got involved in were cases that TG took an interest in; as if the only calls that got through were ones TG *approved* of in some way.

So thought Hank, one way or another, TG would know who 'the prisoner' was. Not that Hank could just come out and ask him. No. The Court of Ghouls, who had assigned TG to the job of keeping an eye on Hank, banned him from giving Hank any obvious help. But Hank imagined that he knew how to play TG; how to pump him for clues, without TG even knowing he was giving anything away.

Hank wandered over to his bed, lay on top of the covers and stared at the ceiling. Sleep would be a long time coming tonight.

# CHAPTER TWO
# A WEE MYSTERY

IT was almost noon the next day before Hank awoke. He rubbed his bleary eyes and looked in the mirror. After all this time, he was still taken aback by his own appearance. Hank had no flesh on his face or on his bones either, for that matter. He looked around for his special 'potion'. He was not finding it easy being 'dead and unburied' in Glasgow.

He made his way into his office and stepped back in shock. Seated at the smaller of the two desks, robed from head to toe in black, his red eyes burning like coals, was the Grim Reaper. He still had the power to unnerve Hank.

Hank recovered his composure. "Hey, TG," he smiled. "Looks like you made it out of bed before me for the first time this century! I wonder if you can help me with a wee mystery that's landed in my lap."

A knock on the office door signalled Charlie and Annie's arrival. TG seemed to be mighty glad of the interruption. Helping Hank with his 'wee mystery' didn't appear to be on TG's agenda at the moment. Hank made a mental note of TG's unease.

He poured himself a strong, black coffee and nodded a greeting in the kids' direction. TG merely raised an eyebrow. Charlie sat down on the big leather couch and Annie perched on her favourite window seat.

Sometimes Annie was so quiet that the others forgot she was even in the room. Charlie and Annie were brother and sister; Charlie being the eldest at twelve while Annie was two years younger.

Annie had taken to following Charlie around. Not that she found him particularly interesting but it was a lot more fun than doing all the girlie things most of her friends did. Detecting had never interested her until she and Charlie had helped Hank solve his first case in Glasgow. While it had scared her senseless, she had found the buzz of solving a case hard to match and she now admitted to herself that she had become as hooked as Charlie.

Having something in common with her brother bothered her – but not as much as being bored did. She had discovered Charlie's links with Hank during Hank's first case in Glasgow. One way or another, she had managed to get herself involved in their crime solving adventures. Though Charlie would have *died* rather than admit it, he had developed a grudging admiration for Annie (or 'Ace' as he always called her). Over the last few months as he watched her at work, he had to admit his sister had guts!

"You look terrible, Hank," said Charlie as he reached over and helped himself to a biscuit. "I mean, you never look particularly good," he continued, "but this morning you look gross!"

"Hey, don't hold back, kid," said Hank, reaching for his special potion and taking a large gulp to try and speed up the return of the flesh to his bones.

Annie pulled her legs underneath her on the window seat.

"So, I guess you called 'cause you're stuck on a case and need some expert help?" she said.

Hank was prevented from answering her as the phone started ringing. Hank looked at them all, wondering which of them would answer it. Eventually, Annie picked it up.

"Who was on the phone?" asked Hank, as he watched Annie replace the receiver. Even Charlie looked at Annie expectantly.

"Some weirdo calling himself a prisoner," came the reply.

## CHAPTER THREE
# THE CRANK

THERE were three more of these phone calls before Hank decided to act. A contact at *The Cesspit* lent Hank and TG some sophisticated tracking equipment used in the tracing of crank telephone calls. They set up the equipment in the office and waited. And waited.

Hank was dozing in his office chair with the television turned down low when the call came through. He picked up the receiver, simultaneously pressing the record button on the tracker.

"Hello?"

Yes! There it was again, that same voice uttering the same words.

"Help me! Please, I need you to help me."

Hank sat down, keeping the receiver close to his ear.

"What sort of help do you need?" he asked, trying to stall for time. "What do you want me to do for you? Can you tell me where you are?"

"I'm a prisoner," came the reply. "A prisoner who needs your help."

"Is someone holding you against your will?" asked Hank, wondering if the caller was ever going to get beyond the same plea. "Can you tell me anything about your surroundings, anything that will help?"

"Just help me...please..." replied the voice.

The voice faded and all too soon Hank heard the sound of the dialling tone. He'd lost him. The caller had gone. At least he had the call taped. He'd play it over a couple of times; see if he could pick up any clues. He and Charlie could go over it again tomorrow.

The recording equipment they'd borrowed was sophisticated enough to pick up any background noise. The next day they were able to temporarily block out the caller's voice and concentrate on what had been happening around him when he made the call.

Hank was quickly able to identify the sound of some kind of door closing; it could have been the door of an elevator, or perhaps the whoosh of an automatic door. He couldn't figure out which.

Charlie rewound the tape a few times. There was the noise of something going past on wheels. But what? A child's buggy? A bicycle? Charlie played it again.

"I know this sounds a bit mad, Hank, but it sounds like a supermarket trolley."

Hank nodded. "Yeah right, kid. Like, we got ourselves someone being held captive in Sainsbury's. Someone who has a problem with using the stairs so uses the elevators a lot. I don't think so."

Charlie looked disdainfully at the detective. "I *did* say I knew it sounded mad," he repeated. "Maybe we should start from the beginning again."

A couple of hours later they'd made no more progress and decided they'd have to wait for the next call before they could pick up any more information.

When the next call came through, the background noises were much the same as before. However, this time there was the added noise of drawers, heavy drawers by the sound of things. Twice they were opened and closed and again the sound of what Charlie had thought was a supermarket trolley. Hank switched off the tape.

"It's somewhere big and hollow," said Annie, "like a cave." She had joined Hank and Charlie to see if she could be of any help.

"Yeah," Charlie reluctantly agreed, "everything has an echo." He looked at Hank.

"It's *not* a supermarket, Charlie," said Hank.

"A warehouse, then," suggested Charlie. "Big, lots of things being wheeled about, drawers being opened and closed. Yeah, makes sense to me, " he said defiantly.

"I'm not convinced," said Hank. "Where does the elevator noise come in? You don't usually find them in warehouses."

Charlie shrugged. "You could do, Hank. Anyway, who says it's definitely the noise of an elevator?"

Annie raised her hand, as though she were in class. Hank looked over at her.

"Did either of you guys notice how the caller lowers his voice each time one of those trolley things passes by?" she said. "I mean, it's not like the sound of the trolley drowns him out, more like he speaks more quietly."

Charlie looked unimpressed, as he always did when upstaged by his kid sister.

"Well, perhaps that's because our friend doesn't want anyone to overhear his cranky little calls," he suggested dismissively.

"I don't know, Charlie," Annie persisted. "He seems to speak in hushed tones, both when there are trolleys passing and when drawers are being opened and closed."

Charlie shook his head. "You're off on the wrong tack, Ace. Let it go, the guy just doesn't want to be overheard. Some kind of crank probably."

Hank looked more thoughtful. "I don't know, Charlie. Let's think about this for a minute. Aside from supermarkets and warehouses, think of a large, *cavernous* building where our friend could be making these calls from?"

"Large, *what* building?" asked Annie, quietly. She was clever. She knew that. But that didn't mean that she knew what every big word meant. She made a mental note to look it up later. Knowing even one word less than Charlie annoyed her!

Charlie ignored her and tried to answer Hank's question.

"An empty school hall?" he suggested. "A church?"

Hank nodded. "And just how many supermarket trolleys have you seen recently inside a church?"

Charlie looked thoughtful.

"A hospital?" said Annie, rejoining the conversation.

Hank smiled. "Now we're getting somewhere. Can you be a bit more specific?"

"A *mortuary!*" breathed Annie, her eyes wide.

Hank sighed with more than a little sense of relief. Bingo! He thought to himself. Of course he'd worked out that it was a mortuary right from the beginning but part of his brief from the Court Of Ghouls was to train Charlie in how to solve cases – and solve them honestly at that.

But it was frustrating for him, having relied solely on his own gut instincts for so long, to have to guide Charlie by the hand from clue to clue. Okay, Charlie had been getting better at detecting as the last cases had shown but sometimes he was more interested in 'being a detective' than 'solving the case'.

Hank knew deep down that without Annie's

help Charlie wouldn't get there. However, himself and Annie *together*, made a good team; her instincts and Charlie's boundless energy and enthusiasm.

Hank stood up, took a swig of his flesh-restoring potion, grabbed his hat from its stand and opened the office door.

"All right," he said to Charlie and Annie over his shoulder. "Let's start at the nearest hospital."

CHAPTER FOUR

# WELL GENIUS...

THE huge, imposing hospital cast a shadow over the nearby buildings. Large sections of the hospital were in disrepair; the walls were cracked, paint peeled from windows and there was an overall atmosphere of gloom and despair.

Hank, Charlie and Annie entered via the visitors' car park, dodging cars which were being driven too quickly and erratically by visitors leaving. Visitors who were pleased to have done their duty and visited their loved ones, but even more pleased to be escaping.

Hank pushed the rotating door and the three of them made their way towards one of the hospital corridors. Visitors walked to and from the wards, some carrying fruit and flowers. Patients were being wheeled past on wheelchairs, perhaps on their way back to their ward, perhaps to theatre. The constant stream of people passing meant that no one paid any attention to Hank, Charlie and Annie.

They seemed to have walked for miles. Each

time they turned a corner another never-ending corridor faced them and another set of confusing directions was displayed on a board above their heads. Eventually, towards the back of the hospital, Annie spotted the sign for the mortuary.

"There, Hank, look," she said, trying to contain her excitement.

Hank nodded. He'd spotted it too.

"Okay, kids, here's what we need to do. It's just starting to get dark outside, so we'll kill some time in the cafeteria till night falls. Then I have to plant myself in the mortuary." He looked at Charlie. "And no wisecracks about that being where I really belong."

"But what are you going to do once you're in there, Hank? What if we're wrong? What if the caller isn't here at all?" asked Annie.

"Our job right now, Annie," said Hank, "is to gather clues and we gotta start somewhere. You can't solve a case without clues. The case solving comes at the end. Don't be impatient, guys. We're only at the beginning."

Hank ushered the two in the direction of the cafeteria.

"If he doesn't show up here tonight, we'll come back another night. And another and another, till we find our man." He began to fidget at a vending machine. "Now, what do you guys want to drink?"

Half an hour later, Hank decided it was time to get the show on the road. Though they'd been able to wander freely around the hospital corridors, Hank knew the staff wouldn't take too kindly to them hanging about the mortuary! They would have to be careful.

They walked in single file up the long corridor, trying to keep close to the wall and appear as unobtrusive as possible. A woman wearing a white coat, which looked as though it hadn't seen the inside of a washing machine for some time, rushed past. She paid no heed to the three of them; too intent on reading the notes on the clipboard she was carrying.

To get inside the mortuary, it was necessary to leave the hospital and go outside into the grounds. A sign hung above the entrance of the mortuary; suspended from a rusty chain it blew backwards and forwards in the wind. The 'M' was missing so that the sign read 'ortuary'. No one had bothered to fix it and Hank didn't suppose anyone ever would. It was only dead bodies they were taking down there, after all, and they weren't gonna complain!

A small flight of steps curled round and down into the mortuary, deep in the bowels of the hospital. The entrance was dark; the single light bulb there being totally inadequate for its purpose. The entrance was fairly low and Hank had to remove his hat so that he could get through.

"You wait here," he whispered. "I'll give this place the once over and I'll be back as quick as I can."

He disappeared and Charlie checked his watch. 10:15. If Hank wasn't back in an hour, he was going in. No matter what his instructions were.

He signalled to Annie to follow him. There was an overgrown garden on their right hand side. Trees and bushes had been left to their own devices but for Charlie and Annie's purpose of concealing themselves, it was almost perfect. They found an old garden seat and sat down. Annie pulled her jacket more tightly around her as the night had suddenly grown cold.

Inside, Hank was making his way precariously down the stairs. There must be another entrance, Hank thought, no one could possibly get a dead body down this narrow staircase – at least not without breaking their own neck!

Finally he entered a small room. The smell was the first thing that struck him. Death. He should have been used to it by now; he had been in the Grim Reaper's company often enough but it was just one of those smells you never quite got accustomed to.

He tried to take short breaths and inhale as little as possible. He opened a door and found himself in a huge ward. Each side of the ward was lined with trolleys on which lay the bodies of recently dead people, each body discreetly covered by a white hospital sheet. Hank looked towards the opposite end of the room.

There were sets of drawers, rows and rows of them. Hank wondered if they, too, contained bodies. He was just about to start walking towards the drawers to investigate when he heard it.

It was a whooshing noise, like that of elevator doors opening. He stepped back, quickly flattening himself against the wall, managing to squeeze his body between a trolley and a tall, upright medical cabinet.

He turned his head in the direction the noise had come from and tried to see in the half-light. He had been right. There *was* another entrance. Leading straight from the hospital itself.

Himself, Charlie and Annie had come in the wrong way. This was obviously the easiest way for intruders to get into the mortuary!

The doors to the elevator, which had descended from the upper floors down to the mortuary, closed with a whoosh. A mortuary attendant stood on the top of the two steps which would bring him down into the ward where Hank was hiding.

He carried a torch, which Hank thought strange. Didn't any of the lights work in here? The attendant wore pale blue trousers and matching shirt; he had soft shoes on his feet.

He began to walk along the opposite side of the ward to where Hank was, stopping occasionally at one of the bodies to shine his torch and check a tag, which hung from a protruding toe. He did this all the way up the ward and Hank was grateful for the semi-darkness.

Only now the attendant was beginning to come down the other side of the ward and Hank had nowhere to escape to! How could he explain his presence? He tried to disappear further and further into the wall, wishing yet again that he had perfected the art of disappearing. The footsteps came closer, then, suddenly, he heard once again the whoosh of the elevator doors.

"Johnny? Are you down there, Johnny?" came a voice from the far end of the ward.

Johnny looked up at the man who had shouted down to him. "Yeah, I'm here, what is it?"

"You're needed upstairs. Carson's looking for you."

Johnny sighed, switching off the torch. "Okay, I'll be right with you," he said, straightening the sheet on the body nearest to him and looking slightly reluctant to leave the mortuary.

Hank wouldn't allow himself to breathe a sigh of relief. Not just yet.

When the elevator doors closed and the two attendants returned to the main part of the hospital, Hank allowed himself to move. His left arm was jammed firmly against the side of the cabinet and he had to be careful not to knock it over as he tried to free himself.

He'd make his way back upstairs for now. Charlie and Annie would wonder where he was. He'd seen enough for now, anyway, though he'd have been happier if 'Johnny' had said a bit more. He hadn't spoken quite enough for Hank to figure out if he and the 'prisoner' on the phone were one and the same.

He stooped to climb back up the stairs and noticed an ID tag lying on the floor. It must have fallen from one of the bodies. He picked it up and put it in his pocket.

He walked back up the stairs and out the door. He soon spotted Charlie and Annie seated on the garden bench and went over to join them.

The night was quiet and his feet crunched the leaves underfoot.

He told them what had happened in the mortuary, saying he'd need to pay another visit. He hadn't got nearly enough information.

"But you must have found something, Hank, some sort of clue?" asked Charlie.

Hank remembered the tag and took it out of his pocket.

"Nearly forgot this," he said. "An ID tag that must have fallen from one of the bodies."

"What use is that?" asked Annie

"It's a clue, Ace," answered Charlie.

"'It's a clue, *Annie!*" said Annie.

"Whatever. It's a clue."

"Thank you Charlie, without you pointing out the extremely obvious, where would we be?"

Hank let them quarrel for a few seconds before dangling the ID tag in front of them.

"Either of you geniuses want to look at the clue? Or do you just wanna argue about it?"

Charlie noted the impatience in Hank's voice and apologised. Hank handed the ID tag to Charlie. He flipped it over and read the name written on it. He gasped.

"Well, Sherlock, what does it say?" asked Annie sarcastically.

Charlie looked up at her, his face white with shock, and said:

"Charlie Christian."

CHAPTER FIVE

# THE DEAD HERRING

"IT'S probably a coincidence, Charlie, don't worry," panted Annie as she ran to try to keep up with her brother. Trying to comfort her brother was a new experience for Annie and she wasn't much good at it. She felt daft saying something so obviously unconvincing but what else could she do? After trying several lines, she decided that making light of it might help.

"If it's any comfort, bro, you don't look dead. Smell dead, maybe, but…"

Hank gave her a look which clearly said, "quit while you're not ahead". She shut up.

Hank wanted to say very little on the subject of the ID tag at this stage. Of course he'd known that the name on the tag had been that of his young friend, Charlie Christian, but he hadn't yet worked out why. He was more than a little concerned. Coincidence was not something Hank was a great believer in.

"Maybe somebody knows we're moving in the right direction," he said.

"What makes you say that?" asked Annie after

a pause. She had waited to let Charlie answer but he was still too gob-smacked from reading his own name on the ID tag.

"Perhaps we were meant to find that tag," suggested Hank.

"You mean we've been thrown a dead herring?" asked Annie.

"It's a *red* herring, Annie. And I said, perhaps. Maybe we're meant to be scared off the case, " said Hank, looking at Charlie.

Charlie strode along in front of them, his head down, his hands pushed deep into his pockets. Hank went back to his office and Charlie and Annie made their way home.

The warmth of the kitchen welcomed them as they opened the door to their home. Charlie shrugged off his jacket and threw it into his bedroom. He sat down heavily on a kitchen chair.

He hadn't spoken a word since the ID tag had been shown to him, other than mumbling, "Sure" to Annie as she repeated. "Don't worry..."

Annie sat down on the chair opposite him. She said nothing, realising now that the best way to help Charlie gather his thoughts was for her to stay silent.

Charlie was spooked. "What do you think it means, Ace? First of all some weirdo calls Hank's office, then puts my name on the body of a dead person."

Ace nodded slowly. "I know what you mean, Charlie, it's just that I can't make sense of it for now." She glanced at the clock. "It's late, maybe we should get some sleep and look at the facts again in the morning."

"Okay," Charlie agreed. "We'll head over to Hank's first thing tomorrow, no point in trying to figure things out tonight."

They went down the hall together and into their bedrooms. Annie fell asleep almost instantly but Charlie lay awake into the early hours of the morning. Sleep, when it came, brought with it vivid dreams of dead bodies for sale on supermarket shelves; with broken and creaky signs hanging above them, each of them giving an anagram of his name.

He was still tired when he reached Hank's office but he and Annie climbed the stairs quickly, keen to look again at the clues and get to the bottom of the case.

Hank was up and about and had typed up (using two fingers) the transcript of the previous two telephone conversations. He placed them on the desk, along with the ID tag. The tag was face down.

Charlie placed the tag face-up on the desk and grinned. "No point in hiding the facts, Hank, better to face your fears."

Hank nodded. "Okay, Charlie, let's get on with it then. Let's look at the clues in the order in which they came."

Lunchtime came and went unnoticed, so intent were they on trying to find some as yet unnoticed clue.

The telephone rang and Hank picked it up.

"Help me," came the plea again. Hank was instantly alert. "It's him," he mouthed to Charlie and Annie, motioning to them to hit the record button.

"Look," began Hank, firmly. "I'm perfectly willing to help you, that's what I'm here for, but unless you can give me some more clues…"

"More clues?" returned the voice. "I thought you were a detective, Mr Kane? How many more clues do you need? You seemed to be on the right track last night?"

Hank looked at Charlie and Annie. So the caller was watching them. "If you are where I think you are, why can't you simply walk out on your own? Why do you need me?"

"Ah Mr Kane, there are so many things you simply don't understand," came the reply. "I need *your* help, I need *you* to come to *me*."

Once again, the caller hung up before Hank had satisfied himself that he had asked enough questions.

"It's like you said last night, Hank," began Charlie. "You're going to have to go back into the mortuary."

Hank nodded in agreement. "Yeah, but this time I'll be one of the bodies on the trolleys. This time I'll be going in as a stiff."

## CHAPTER SIX

# A NIGHT AT THE MORTUARY

HANK decided the best way back into the mortuary was the way they had entered the previous night. They waited for nightfall and set off. Annie wasn't entirely convinced that the plan would work but Charlie persuaded her that it was the best shot they had. He then asked her if she had any better suggestions. She hadn't, so she decided to keep quiet.

Quite simply, Hank was planning to spend the entire night in the mortuary, pretending to be dead. But he *was* dead, Annie reasoned to herself, though not quite in the same way the rest of the bodies in the mortuary were. She pondered for a moment, thought about involving Charlie in her thought process, then decided against it. It was all just too confusing she decided, best just to leave well enough alone.

Charlie and Annie were to leave Hank alone in the mortuary and not get in the way. Neither were they to hang about outside. Hank told them to meet him in the overgrown garden at nine o'clock the following morning. Hopefully by that time he'd have something to report back to them.

He removed his hat and once again descended the narrow stairs. The clock outside was striking and Hank counted ten chimes as he arrived back inside the ward.

He wished he'd remembered to bring nose plugs. The stench of death was overwhelming. He suddenly realised he'd forgotten something else – his flesh-restoring potion! He'd stick out like a sore thumb next to these dead guys if anyone were to see his skeletal frame. After all, these bodies hadn't even decomposed yet, let alone dropped the flesh from their bones. He'd have to keep himself well hidden, covered with the hospital sheet at all times.

Luckily for him there was some space tonight. Last time he'd been inside the mortuary it'd been jam-packed! Some bodies had obviously been taken away for post mortem examinations, others to be buried. Whatever the reason, there were a few trolleys vacant and Hank chose the one nearest the back of the ward. He was hoping the 'prisoner' as he liked to call himself would venture into the mortuary tonight, make another phone call and Hank would catch him red-handed.

Two hours later, Hank was bored senseless. Nothing. He was becoming restless. He turned on his side, then turned onto his other side, then eventually onto his back.

He stared up at the ceiling, able to make out the numerous cracks as his eyes grew accustomed to the darkness. He replayed all the facts of the case in his head. He couldn't think of anything new to add to what was already known about the case. He sighed, and then tried to stifle it in case anyone heard. He almost laughed out loud. In case anyone heard? He was in a mortuary with a bunch of stiffs. Who was going to hear? He decided to give it another hour or so then leave. There was no point in wasting his entire night.

Charlie motioned to Annie to move forward. "Shh," he said, as he put his hand to his lips in a silent gesture. Annie raised her eyebrows. Like she didn't know she had to be quiet! Her brother drove her nuts sometimes!

Despite Hank's request to the contrary, Charlie and Annie had stayed in the hospital grounds, awaiting darkness. Charlie didn't like the idea of Hank solving a case on his own. They were a team and they would solve this case together.

He and Annie climbed down the last of the steps into the mortuary and felt their way along the side of a wall until Charlie's hands found a wooden cupboard. It was empty except for a shelf full of creams, potions and syringes. If they were careful, they could conceal themselves inside.

Charlie slid the doors open and both of them climbed inside. Hot, sticky and cramped, Annie could have thought of plenty of other places she'd like to be, but said nothing. If Charlie could spend hours locked up in here, then so could she.

They didn't have long to wait. The cupboard had a glass panel which ran along the top. If Charlie stood on tiptoe, he could just about peer outside and see what was going on in the ward. The lift doors opened and closed with the by now familiar whooshing sound.

Charlie tried to keep his head down, without losing sight of who was coming into the mortuary.

A dark haired man wearing regulation hospital trousers and shirt came out of the lift. He was followed by a smaller man with glasses, dressed in similar clothes. The taller of the two attendants stepped back and indicated that the other should move forward. "This way," he said. "The supplies are in the cabinet at the far end of the room."

Charlie drew in his breath sharply. "The cabinet at the far end of the room?" But that was where he and Annie were hiding. They had to get out of here, and fast. But how? He tried to stay calm. Maybe Hank would overhear and create a diversion. But Hank didn't know they were here! Hank thought they were at home safely tucked up in bed!

A scuttling noise in the mortuary stopped the smaller attendant from walking any further.

"What was that?" he asked, his voice shaky. He was obviously new to the job.

The first attendant stopped and laughed. "Place is full of rats. Don't worry, you'll get used to them. They're probably more afraid of you than you are of them."

"Rats?" The man was appalled. He held his clipboard protectively in front of him, placing his feet very carefully on the stone floor.

Something else scuttled along the floor and again he stopped in his tracks.

"Don't be stupid," said the taller attendant. "They won't harm you. Look." He stamped his feet really hard on the floor and a rat flew quickly from under a bed and made its way to the relative darkness of the stairwell.

Charlie and Annie took their chance. Both men's eyes were on the other side of the room. Each time the attendant stamped his feet, he laughed and pointed at small, scuttling furry creatures, which ran for cover. The rats were relatively young and not yet fearless enough to stand their ground.

Charlie slid the door of the cupboard open and he and Annie slid out. Charlie signalled to Annie that they should make for the trolley directly across from them and clamber underneath. Luckily for them the sheet covering the dead body was long and hung over the side of the bed, offering them some cover at least.

The attendants continued on their way up the ward. The newer of the two was more than a little afraid, keeping to the centre of the room, his eyes darting to the right and left, taking in his surroundings. He hated the smell and didn't think that he'd ever get used to it. On some of the beds he could just about make out the outline of the corpses, on others arms had fallen out and hung over the side. The whole feel of the place gave him the creeps. He didn't think he'd be staying long in the job.

The door to the cupboard was still open. Charlie and Annie hadn't had time to close it. The attendant paused briefly, shook his head as though trying to remember if he himself had left it open. He shrugged and pulled open both doors.

As he did so, a noise from just behind them caused the new attendant to turn around. The sight he saw would live with him for the rest of his life.

From the bed opposite there came a groaning noise, then the sheet began to move and fall from the body. Though mainly white, areas of the skin on the corpse were blackened, partially due to the cause of death and partially because death itself was taking over the body. The eyes were wide open, staring, and the corpse sat upright in the bed, leaning towards the terrified man.

As the corpse sat up, the sheet covering it rose up with it. This was the trolley that Charlie and Annie were hiding under. They found themselves revealed.

The taller of the attendants had turned to reassure the other man, to tell him that this often happened with bodies which weren't that long dead. Suddenly he spotted two children trying desperately to conceal themselves. He moved forward.

It couldn't be, could it? He looked again, trying to get a better look at Charlie and Annie's faces. "Hey, you two, what are you doing in here?"

Charlie and Annie scampered out from their hiding place, falling over each other in their haste to get out. They dragged one another up the stairs, falling and clutching onto one another as they ran. The attendant followed, running as fast as he could, shouting after them to come back.

But he wasn't as fit as he used to be and Charlie and Annie were too quick for him. By the time he got to the top of the stairs they were completely out of sight. He paused, wheezing, leaning against the side of the door trying to get his breath back. He wiped the sweat from his brow and began his descent back into the mortuary.

He'd get them next time, he reassured himself. And what the heck had they been doing in the mortuary anyway!

Next morning, Hank re-checked his watch. 9:20 am. Charlie and Annie were late. Probably overslept. He pulled his hat down over his face. He'd have to leave soon, he didn't want anyone to glimpse him in his present skeletal form. He got up from the garden bench and pulled his coat collar up as far as it would go.

"Kids," he muttered to himself as he began the walk home on his own. "Couldn't ever rely on them to be on time."

After all, he was the one who'd been out all night. He was the one who'd been working, stuck in the mortuary with nothing but a bunch of corpses for company. He stifled a yawn as he walked.

"Ah well," he smiled to himself. "Best night's sleep I've had in a long time!"

## CHAPTER SEVEN

# CONFESSION

HANK was surprised to see both Charlie and Annie waiting for him at his office, both of them looking just a little bit shaken! He took off his hat and coat, poured himself a coffee and sat down.

"What happened to you two? I waited for you outside the mortuary but you didn't bother to show. Did you oversleep? Or do you have a *good* reason for not turning up as instructed?"

Charlie and Annie looked at one another. Annie indicated that Charlie should speak. She preferred that Charlie admit to Hank that they hadn't gone straight home last night, as he'd instructed.

Charlie decided to play for time. "How was your night, Hank? Did you spend the entire evening in the mortuary? Did anything unusual happen?"

Hank stirred some sugar into his coffee. "Nothing at all," he smiled slowly. "A very peaceful night, actually. Didn't hear a thing."

Charlie and Annie glanced at one another.

"And you didn't see any mortuary attendants, hear scuttling rats, see dead bodies sit upright? No loud screaming, no lift doors opening and closing, no feet running up stairs?"

"Not a thing," replied Hank, as he switched from sipping his coffee to swigging his flesh-restoring potion. Better get some meat back on his bones!

He looked at Charlie and Annie suspiciously.

"Why do you ask? Do you guys know something I don't?" he said, teasing what he already knew to be the truth out of Charlie

Charlie sighed wearily. "We were there, Hank," he said, putting up his hand to stop the detective protesting. "Yes, I know you told us to go home but we decided against it and joined you in the mortuary. Just as well, actually, at least Ace and I managed to stay awake."

Hank looked indignant.

"Okay, Charlie, so I was a bit tired," he said, pretending that he had indeed fallen asleep and missed everything. "Now if you don't mind, I'd like to know exactly what went on last night."

Charlie and Annie told him the whole story, finishing with them clambering up the stairs to escape the two attendants. They had decided it would be too dangerous to hang about the garden, so came straight to Hank's office. Hank shook his head.

"I told you it wasn't safe. I told you to go home, didn't I?" He looked from one to the other.

Charlie shrugged and tried to protest. "We were only trying to be helpful, Hank...." He tailed off, the look on Hank's face told him he'd said enough.

Annie kept her bare wrist hidden underneath the desk and hoped Charlie wouldn't notice. The watch her mum had given her for her last birthday was missing. It had been on her wrist last night when she went out and now it wasn't. She must have dropped it in the mortuary.

She decided to keep her mouth shut and not let Hank or Charlie know. She'd get it herself, as soon as possible. She'd go back to the mortuary, alone. Scary? Yeah. Scarier than telling Mum she'd lost her watch? Yeah, too right!

Worse, she'd have to confess to Hank that she hadn't noticed her own watch was missing. That wouldn't help her growing reputation with Hank as a pretty good detective. And, worst of all, Charlie would enjoy feeling superior to her, even if it was just for a moment.

## CHAPTER EIGHT

# THE COLLECTOR

JOHNNY Demetrio lined up the jars in front of him, the labels facing towards him. Some of the labels had almost frozen over so he had to rub the ice away with his fingers. It had taken him a long time, and a lot of patience but he'd done it. There was only one thing missing.

Demetrio (or Johnny Deadbeat as he was known) was nothing if not patient. He'd hatched his plan years previously, plotted everything exactly and executed each stage with precision. Both his parents were dead. Both of them had died after long and painful illnesses and Johnny had decided when his mother had breathed her last that he wasn't going to suffer the same fate.

He'd started off working as a night porter in the local hospital, graduating to the post of first junior, and now senior mortuary attendant. He'd learnt a lot about the human body during his work at the hospital and was allowed to stay and watch the odd post mortem, depending on which pathologist was carrying it out. In death, the human body was horrible, decaying rapidly, rotting almost beneath the pathologist's hands. Johnny became even more determined that death would not claim him.

He had started to make plans for his own eternal life. He collected livers freshly cut from bodies, hearts which no longer kept beat, brains which were as dead as the bodies they came from. He collected every organ he thought would come in useful and took them home.

He put the organs on ice, packed them tightly and stored them on the top shelf of his freezer. These were his transplant organs, the ones that would be used to keep him alive in any eventuality. In his deranged mind, he could see nothing wrong with the plan and couldn't quite grasp the fact that the organs would be of no use to him.

And even when the truth dawned on him, as it did from time to time, he convinced himself that he'd think of something. Some magic potion perhaps.

And now, the final piece of the jigsaw. He had to get blood. And it had to be fresh, young blood that he could store for himself. His blood type was rare and though he had seen the odd sample of it very occasionally in the hospital, the blood had come from old people, people who were practically staring death in the face.

Johnny didn't want their blood. He wanted the blood of a young person, someone young and vibrant whose blood would flow through his veins and refresh and regenerate him.

And very recently he had discovered someone who possessed that very blood type. Someone who had fallen and cut their leg and been to the hospital to have stitches. Johnny had conveniently been around to clean up the blood soaked wipes and bandages the nurses had used. He'd even managed to check the records to find out the girl's name.

Annie Christian.

Once Johnny had that information, it had been a simple case of figuring out how to get the girl to the mortuary in order to get more of her blood. He'd followed her, discovered where she spent most of her time and that her brother liked to think of himself as a sort of apprentice detective. The older guy who seemed to be in charge of the whole detective agency operation was a bit strange. Johnny hadn't seen him up close just yet but the guy had a weird aura about him and a faint smell that was vaguely familiar to Johnny.

So he had started to make the strange phone calls. These detectives were all the same, he thought, liked to think of themselves as some kind of heroes. Johnny knew if he pestered them long enough they'd come looking for him. Trying to help him. Ha! If only they knew.

Added to that he'd had Charlie's name written on one of the corpse's ID tags. He knew that'd spook them! He'd counted on them thinking that someone was trying to scare them off. He had guessed enough about the weird trio of detectives to know that such tactics would not scare them but instead simply arouse their curiosity even more.

And now he had the girl's watch. That bit wasn't planned. No, that was sheer luck. But Johnny convinced himself that he deserved such luck. He'd lured her into his trap and she'd fallen and snagged her watch, leaving it behind when she ran so swiftly from the mortuary the previous night. Johnny knew from examining the rest of the watch that it was fairly new and he also knew that Annie would be back for it.

And when she came back, he'd be waiting.

## CHAPTER NINE
# THE LIE

CHARLIE played one of the tapes over again.

"That's him, Hank, I'm pretty sure of it. I heard him speak last night and I'd swear that's the same voice."

Annie nodded. "Charlie's right, Hank. It's definitely the same person who's been calling you."

Hank looked thoughtful. He was glad Charlie and his kid sister were picking up on the clues. And he wasn't helping them *too* much. All he was doing was asking the obvious questions detectives would ask.

"Buy why?" he wondered aloud, "Why pretend you're being held captive and make crank calls? I don't get it."

"Maybe there's nothing to get," said Charlie. "Maybe the guy's a fruitcake, pure and simple. Maybe he gets his kicks from making weird phone calls. Who knows?"

Hank didn't seem so sure. He had to decide what to do next. Wait for yet another crank call, or pay the mortuary attendant another visit?

Charlie had a dental appointment and stood up to leave. "I've got to go, Hank. You coming, Annie?"

She nodded. "What will we do, Hank?" she asked.

"Let's meet back here tomorrow," said Hank. "Leave things as they are for tonight. You guys must be exhausted. Do what you have to do today then go home and get a good night's rest. Meet me back here at ten o'clock tomorrow morning and we'll take things from there – if you turn up this time that is."

Charlie buttoned up his jacket and stifled a yawn. He *was* tired and so was Annie. He looked at his sister. She looked very pale but he thought she also looked worried. In an uncharacteristic display of brotherly love, he opened the door for her and allowed her to go first. She walked in front and pushed her untidy hair back from her eyes.

Seeing the gesture, Charlie noticed that her watch was missing. "Where's your watch, Annie?" he asked.

"At home," Annie replied quickly. "I forgot to put it on before I left yesterday morning."

Charlie nodded. "Strange," he thought. She must have really been in a hurry. That watch was her pride and joy. It had been ever since Mum gave it to her as a birthday present.

His sister walked ahead of him, her head down, face blushing at the lie she had just told. Charlie waved goodbye to Hank and closed the door behind him. They walked along Gordon Street and took a left, heading off to catch a bus, which would take them home.

## CHAPTER TEN
# HELLO JOHNNY

ANNIE lay down on top of her bed, put her CD player on repeat and closed her eyes. The music lulled her and she slept for most of the afternoon. When she woke it was almost nightfall again; that strange time between daylight and dusk when the world seems quieter than usual and streetlights cast eerie glows.

She got up and went into the bathroom. She had a quick shower, dressed and checked Charlie's room. His faint, sleeping shape was almost visible in the darkness. She pulled on her jacket and left the house.

It was chilly outside and she walked quickly towards the bus stop. She got on the first bus that came along and, a few stops later, got off at the hospital.

She wondered which was her best route. If she went in through the front hospital entrance it was less scary. However she couldn't risk bumping into one of the attendants when she tried to take the lift down to the mortuary. How would she explain her presence? No, far better to enter from the back, she decided. Scary it may be, but it was probably the best way to avoid meeting somebody she didn't want to meet.

She shivered, it was really chilly now, but she knew she was also shivering because she was afraid. She tried to put her fears behind her and entered the mortuary, descending the now familiar steps.

The bodies had been moved again and for a minute she was thrown. The bed they had hidden under the previous night was no longer there. Some sort of cabinet stood in its place. She stood for a minute, her eyes adjusting to the half darkness and tried to get her bearings.

The cupboard she and Charlie had concealed themselves in was where it had been. She thought so anyway. She wasn't sure now. She was getting more and more confused. "Stop," she said to herself, aware of the rising panic she was feeling. She tried to calm herself.

A sudden thump scared her half to death. She jumped and tried to stifle a cry. A hand had fallen from underneath the sheet which covered it. A hand and part of the corpse's upper torso was now visible. The skin was strangely see-through, shiny and more like paper than flesh. She forced her eyes to look away.

She had brought a tiny flashlight with her and now she took it from her pocket and bent down to begin her search. The smell of death assailed her nostrils and it took all her courage to crawl underneath beds, shining the flashlight, hoping against hope that she would find her watch. Six beds later, she had found nothing.

She straightened up and decided to head for the stairs. Who knows, perhaps her watch had fallen off when she and Charlie had begun their frantic escape. If it wasn't there she was going to leave, confess her loss to Charlie and ask him to come back with her.

She bent down on all fours and crawled about the dirty floor, flashlight in hand. The back of the stairs was positioned so that the light didn't help to any great extent so she took to running her hands over the floor, feeling for anything which felt familiar. She tried to ignore the scuttling noises and shook off the tiny spiders, which crawled over her hands.

She was just about to give up when her hand

felt something different. Something hard and shiny, like leather. She felt further. Shoe laces.

She staggered to her feet quickly, dropping the flashlight in her haste. One of the mortuary attendants stood in front of her. It was the elder of the two. She didn't know what to say. She tried desperately to think of an excuse for being there but nothing came quickly to mind. She stood there, struck suddenly dumb.

Johnny just smiled menacingly.

"This what you're looking for, Annie?" he said quietly, dangling her watch in his hand.

## CHAPTER ELEVEN

# THE DONOR

IN Hank's office the next morning Hank, TG and Charlie discussed events.

"But I don't *know* Hank. That's what I'm trying to tell you. She didn't come downstairs for breakfast this morning and when I checked her room, she'd already gone. I presumed, wrongly as it turns out, that she'd already left to come here." Charlie was exasperated and more than a little worried.

TG sat with Charlie and Hank at the desk. He knew where Annie was but of course he couldn't tell them. He also knew that if they didn't hurry up and get to her they might be too late.

Charlie looked at him.

"TG, you must know where Annie is."

The Reaper looked back at him, his red eyes burning. He ran his bony fingers along the edge of his scythe. The Court of Ghouls wouldn't be happy if he offered to help but then again he couldn't sit back and watch while Hank and Charlie searched for the girl. He made his decision quickly.

"Hank, you might want to close your ears. I know I'm not meant to help *you* and I know *you're* not meant to help Charlie. But there's nothing in the rule book says *I* can't help him."

Hank put his hands over his ears and wandered into the next room as if he didn't want to know. But he had already worked out the Johnny Deadbeat angle. That's why he'd wanted Charlie and Annie to come back this morning, so he could explain the whole thing and wrap up this unusually easy case.

He'd guessed the other evening that Charlie and Annie would follow him into the mortuary. He'd been sure that they'd be safe in there when he was there, too. But not even Hank's great instincts could have imagined that Annie would lose her watch. If he'd known, he'd have guessed that she'd sneak back for it.

"Guy called Johnny Deadbeat has her," he mumbled. "In the mortuary. You'd better get there quickly, I don't think there's much time to lose."

Charlie turned white. He grabbed his jacket and motioned to Hank to follow. "Come on,

Hank, we can't hang about. We've got to find Ace."

They left the door of the office wide open and ran down the stairs, out into the chill Glasgow air.

Annie's face was wet. She wasn't crying, she told herself, she was tougher than that. There must be some condensation on the ceiling which had dripped down onto her face. She was scared, yes, but she wasn't crying. She wiped her face impatiently, leaving dirty streaks down her cheeks as she did so.

The 'prisoner' had her trapped. How could she have been so stupid? She had fallen right into his trap. She'd disobeyed orders from Hank, ignored everything her brother had said, and now this weirdo had her captured. Worse than that, nobody knew she was here. She looked down at her left wrist. At least she'd got her watch back.

She hadn't gone meekly. She'd kicked and screamed all the way up and down the ward. She'd cried out and protested as he dragged her into a small ante-room behind the stairwell. It made no difference. Johnny Deadbeat had a firm grasp on her; he'd waited too long for this and wasn't going to let her go.

The room was small and there was very little air circulating. The smell of death and rotting flesh permeated Annie's nostrils. She hadn't noticed until now but her captor stank. She didn't know when he'd last washed or how he was allowed to carry out hospital duties. The smell made her want to gag, to run away, escape from this horrible nightmare. Only Johnny seemed to have other plans – she was going nowhere.

Everything was ready for her. In the corner of the tiny room there was a small wooden seat. Leather straps adorned both the arms and the upper part had a restraint.

Johnny Deadbeat forced Annie into it, the straps were fastened and her head was pushed into the restraint. The tears fell freely now and she was unable to keep them in check.

Her eyes darted around. She was unable to move her head because of the restraint but tried to see what she could in the room. Syringes lay in one corner; dirty, used syringes which had probably been used on other bodies. Test tubes with labels bearing names of other blood donors lay discarded on a shelf, the contents being of no use to Johnny. A small trolley bore knives, scalpels and other lethal looking instruments. Annie was unfamiliar with the names but she knew what they could do.

Worst of all, on the top shelf of the trolley, was a test tube that was larger than the others. It was an empty test tube, with a hand-written label stuck onto the side of it. She didn't want to, but she forced herself to read the label.

There were only two words. Her name.

## CHAPTER TWELVE
# ASK A CRAZY QUESTION

HANK and Charlie were sitting down in the hospital cafeteria. They had left Hank's office so quickly they hadn't yet formed a plan. At least that's what Charlie thought. Hank, however, did have a plan. But he knew Charlie had to be the one to solve the case, so he kept his plan up his sleeve, only to be used as a last resort.

Both of them knew by now that Johnny Demetrio was a dangerous opponent. They were both aware that, if they didn't tread very carefully, Annie would be harmed. And that was the last thing they wanted to happen.

Hank drank deeply from his coffee cup and looked at the Charlie. He knew Charlie was worried, and tried to offer words of encouragement.

"We'll get him, kid, don't worry. We'll sort this out. Annie will be okay."

Charlie nodded and stared into his drink.

"I know," he replied. He was itching to go. He knew that Hank's thoughts of holding back and being careful were the more sensible but at the same time he was desperate to find his sister.

71

The cafeteria was busy, both with staff and hospital visitors, and Charlie found the hum of conversation very annoying. People behaving normally were always irritating when your life was anything *but* normal! He looked again at Hank, becoming more and more irritable at the lack of action on the detective's part. Hank put down his coffee cup and leant forward to speak quietly to his apprentice.

"Okay, kid, let's take this slowly. The last thing we want to do is upset our friend, Mr Demetrio. We can't let him know that we're onto him. So, I need you to take the back stairs and I'll come down in the lift. Whichever one of us finds him first asks him a crazy question. Pretend to be the relative of someone who's recently deceased. Like you're looking for their body. Even if he vaguely recognises you, just act confident and throw him with the question. It will make him hesitate for a moment. It's like bluffing. Trust me, I've used the technique. It's a skill all detectives have to develop."

Charlie thought about this. Hank was probably right. Though Demetrio had probably caught a glimpse of Charlie as he escaped the other night, he was fairly sure he hadn't got a proper look. And if Johnny Deadbeat recognised him as the brother of the girl he'd been following, then bluffing was worth a try. He nodded and motioned to Hank to continue talking.

"That's it," concluded Hank. "Get the guy talking. Let's see what he has to say for himself; hope the other one turns up to help and we take it from there. It's called 'buying time'. And never, at any time, do we endanger Annie."

"Great plan, Hank," said Charlie sarcastically. "Like I couldn't have thought of that myself." He knew what Hank's reply would be before he opened his mouth to speak.

"Got any better ideas? Besides, it's not just the plan that wins the day. It's the putting it into actions that counts. Simple ideas done well are the best of all."

Hank drained his coffee cup and got up to leave. Charlie followed. They split up at the exit of the cafeteria and went their separate ways. Whatever happened, neither would leave the mortuary until they had found Annie.

## CHAPTER THIRTEEN

# YOUNG BLOOD

CHARLIE crept down the narrow staircase, taking care not to make any noise. If Demetrio was in the mortuary, he didn't want to warn him of his arrival.

Meantime, from inside the hospital, Hank had been able to find the lift which would bring him to the mortuary. He arrived there just after Charlie did. Acknowledging each other's presence, the two began their search. There was no sign of anyone having been there but both crept painstakingly up either side of the ward; checking under sheets, underneath beds, searching for clues, anything that would tell them that Annie had been there.

They drew a blank. Charlie sat down on the bottom of the stairs and Hank joined him.

"What now?" asked Charlie. Hank shook his head.

"Think kid, think," urged Hank.

"If Johnny Deadbeat is holding her," suggested Charlie, maybe he's taken her away from the hospital. Maybe they're not here at all."

"Nah," said Hank, trying once again to steer Charlie onto the correct clue path. I've got a feeling about this one, kid. I think he'd keep her here. He's hiding here somewhere. I just know he is."

Charlie looked at Hank suspiciously.

"You seem pretty sure Hank," he said

As he spoke, Charlie idly drew a circle in the dirt with the toe of his trainer. But there were other footprints in the dirt. Footprints much smaller than his!

"Look, Hank," he said, jumping up excitedly, trying not to disturb any more dust. "She *is* here! Look at the footprints. I'll bet you anything you like those prints were made by Annie."

Hank agreed. The prints were definitely smaller than both his own and Charlie's. On closer examination, they were able to pick out small, random paw prints which must be embedded into the trainers. It was Annie all right; she had practically forced her mum to buy her trainers with paw prints on the soles, so great was her love of dogs. Charlie had thought the request unbelievably stupid at the time, but now he was eternally grateful.

Hank and Charlie followed the footprints, treading carefully so as not to lose sight of the path. They found themselves facing a tiny doorway at the back of the stairwell. They looked at each other, briefly, then Hank pushed it open. There was no need to warn Charlie to be careful, they were both well aware of the dangers.

Annie's head was slumped forward onto her chest. She was unconscious. Johnny Deadbeat sat in a corner. He turned when his two visitors arrived.

"Ah, Mr Kane! Young Mr Christian! What a pleasure to see you. Come in, come in. You took your time getting here, didn't you?"

"What have you done to my sister?" began Charlie. "How dare you lay a finger on her..."

Demetrio smiled. "Now, now, young, man. I haven't done anything. It's merely a sleeping draught I've given her. The girl was becoming terribly upset, distraught really and I just couldn't have her making all that noise, now could I? So I gave her a teensy little injection, just enough to knock her unconscious. Ah, but she'll be soooo pleased to see you when the drug wears off."

Hank moved forward and went to lift Annie's head.

Demetrio jumped to his feet, pulling a gun from his back pocket.

"Back off, Kane," he snarled menacingly. "I've waited too long for this moment and neither you nor anybody else is going to spoil it for me."

Hank backed off, raising his hands and keeping them in the air. One of the benefits of being dead was that guns and bullets held no fear for him anymore. After all, he *was* already dead! But this was Charlie's case. Walking through a hail of bullets would be easy enough. Taking the gun from Deadbeat would be easier still. Putting Deadbeat through the nearest wall would be fun. But as long as the gun was pointed at Hank, he knew the others were safe.

"Just let the girl go, Johnny. You can have me; you don't need her. Untie her now. Let her go and nobody need know about it. I'll take her place, just let the girl go home."

Demetrio shook his head. "But that's just where you're wrong, Mr Kane. You see I *do* need her. I need her very much. It's her young blood, pulsing through her veins, making her vibrant and youthful. That's what I want, Mr Kane, to be vibrant and youthful. And that's what I'm going to be. With young Annie's help."

"You see those empty phials over there, Mr Kane? They're for Annie's blood. I was about to start taking the blood when you found us."

"You 'aint much of a scientist are you, Johnny," said Hank. "Do you really think that taking Annie's blood will make you immortal or something? Are you crazy?"

"Actually, Kane, I *am* crazy," Johnny said, with a strange amount of pride.

"Well, it wouldn't take Sherlock Holmes to work that out, now would it?"

Hank was trying to keep Johnny's limited attention focused on him.

"But even crazy killers normally have a logic of their own. A warped logic, perhaps. But, you haven't a clue, have you Johnny? No one can live forever. We all have to die sometime…"

"Well, some of us do, Kane. And some of us have to die today!" he said, raising the gun.

"Tell me, Johnny, what was all that stuff about being a 'prisoner'?" said Hank, playing for time.

"Well, let's just say that I know guys like you. Guys who think they are smart. You can't resist a chance to solve a case."

Hank was yawning.

"Wake me up when you get to the bit about 'the prisoner'."

"We're all prisoners, Kane. We're imprisoned in these bodies of ours. We should be free, free to live for as long as our spirit wants to – not when flesh and bone gives up on us, like some old car!"

"But why call me?" asked Hank.

"Like I said, I needed Annie's blood. I knew the kids hung out with you. I knew they thought they were mini Sherlocks. And like I said, I knew you'd bring them straight to me –"

"It's hardly a master plan now, Johnny, is it? But tell me, where did you get my number from. I'm not exactly in the book."

"I'll level with you, Kane, seeing as these are your last moments on earth! One night down here I was working away, sawing open corpses to get at their vital organs. I often sing that song to myself, you know the one? *I Am A Prisoner.*

Anyway I seemed to black out. When I woke up, I was sure I saw a cloaked figure, with a large pole or something, writing on a piece of paper on that table over there. The figure turned round and stared at me with piercing red eyes! I passed out again; with fright I don't mind admitting. So when I came to, I saw the paper was still there – and it said: "Call Hank Kane on this number. He frees prisoners. You already know one of his helpers".

"And you called. Didn't you wonder who that cloaked figure was?" asked Hank.

"What did I care? I immediately made a plan to get you suckers here, or at least Annie here. And it worked! And now, if you'll excuse me, I have to carry out my plan."

Charlie meanwhile was enraged. He *had* to try and get the gun from Demetrio. He wasn't going to stand by and watch his sister be drained of her blood.

A bare light bulb hung in the centre of the

room and Charlie acted quickly. While Demetrio's attention was focused on Hank, Charlie bent and picked up a stone. He threw it at the bulb and watched as it shattered.

Demetrio pulled the trigger of his gun and the sound of the bullet whistling through the air rang out in the silence. The noise awakened Annie and for a minute she was unsure of where she was. Charlie dashed to her side and started to try and untie the straps which held her arms. The cold steel of the gun pressing against his temple stopped him.

"Get up, slowly," said Demetrio, quietly.

Annie nodded at Charlie and mouthed, "I'm okay."

Charlie stood and looked back at Demetrio. "Now go over there and join your friend."

Charlie turned and saw that Hank was down. The bullet had hit its target and Hank lay looking very dead on the floor.

Demetrio used some extra thick parcel tape to gag Charlie's mouth. He tied his hands with rope and forced him to sit on the floor beside Hank.

"We could have done it the easy way, kids, but

you forced my hand. You've left me with no choice. I'll have to take the blood while you both watch."

Annie was terrified but was trying to stay calm for her brother's sake. Johnny got the first syringe ready. The needle seemed huge and Annie tensed waiting for it to pierce her skin. Charlie tried to kick out, tried to free himself of the rope, but his bindings were too tight.

A resounding crack was heard throughout the room, followed by Johnny Deadbeat falling to the floor. A wound on the back of his head spurted blood, his eyes wide open when he fell. From the darkness behind him, the Grim Reaper appeared, red eyes burning, scythe in hand, black cloak flowing to the ground. Charlie had never been so glad to see anyone in his whole life.

TG pulled the tape from Charlie's mouth and none too gently either! "What did you do to him TG?" Charlie managed to ask. "What did you hit him with?"

"Oh, you know," replied TG coyly. He rubbed the tip of his scythe lovingly and Charlie noticed it was coated in blood. "This old thing comes in quite handy sometimes."

"Except that you've gone and solved the case!" Hank said angrily.

"Well excuse me, Hank, but you were…dead?

"You of all 'people' knew I wasn't dead, TG. How can I teach Charlie if you step in at the last minute?"

"But you *had* already solved the case, Hank…"

"Excuse me," interrupted Charlie, "I think *I* solved the case."

"Yeah, whatever, kid," said TG. He turned back to Hank. "What did I do wrong? Oh, don't tell me, Hank, I know what I did wrong – I saved your life! That's what I did wrong."

"That's the whole point, TG. I don't want my life to be saved! I want to pass over to 'Detective Heaven'. I don't want to be immortal! I've done my bit! Now I'll have to go back to the Court Of Ghouls and be condemned to carry out yet another dumb case!"

"Look, Hank," said TG trying to calm him down. "Number one, you already…eh… I mean, Charlie had already solved the case, right? All I did was step in when you looked like you were in trouble. OK?"

"Step in when we had in under control, more like."

"Yeah right," said TG, "like Charlie having a gun at his head was having things 'under control'?"

"I was playing dead. I was gonna creep up on him…"

"Well, all I did was save you the trouble. Look, it's done. I'll keep it out of my report to the Ghouls, OK. They'll never know. Trust me."

Hank went over to Charlie who had been untying Annie while they'd been arguing.

Charlie wondered how on earth the police would explain scythe wounds and the missing murder weapon! He smiled to himself. He untied Annie as quickly as he could, hugged her then turned to Hank.

"Can I ask a question?" ventured Charlie.

"Sure, go ahead," replied TG.

"How did you get in here?"

"Let's just say that mortuaries are more than familiar to me. I am the Grim Reaper after all! I've brought hundreds of newly dead souls to mortuaries all over the world. I sometimes have to show them their bodies to convince them that they are dead."

Just then Annie stood up and shook her groggy head.

"TG?" she asked

"Yes, Annie?" said TG, "come on, walk and talk. Let's get outta here."

"Does that mean that you personally meet everyone when they die? 'Cause if you do, then how come you can be every where at once?" said Annie, walking with Hank and Charlie's help.

"Well Annie, I'm glad you're back to your old self! Let's just say I've worked it out so that no one is left out."

"But how?" she pressed.

Hank piped up.

"My guess is that the enterprising Grim Reaper has a bunch of helpers around the world. Dead guys like me probably, who help him. Something like that?"

TG grinned. He continued to walk slightly ahead, constantly checking to ensure they were not seen. He'd let Hank and the kids explain all this to the police.

"Let's just say I know how to market a good idea. Call it a franchise operation. Call it global. Call it just plain good business. I've been doing this job for so long that I got tired doing it all by myself. So I have offices in every major city in the world! I employ thousands of… yeah Hank, dead guys like you."

"I've never seen an office anywhere!" said Charlie suspiciously.

"Yeah, like I'd be in the Yellow Pages, kid," said TG.

Annie was now walking ahead on her own. She had recovered well. Like Hank had said, Johnny was no scientist. Whatever concoction he'd given her had completely worn off. They approached the street, TG still squinting ahead to make sure he could avoid contact with people.

"My guess," said Annie, talking a little like Hank, "is that you can only find your offices if you are invited to them. Like when we look for Hank's office. We can't find it unless Hank has called us, or told us to meet him there."

Hank was laughing quietly as they all stood

in the doorway, waiting for TG to give the all clear.

"You have me sussed," said TG, completely unconcerned.

CHAPTER FOURTEEN

# THE VERDICT

THE Court of Ghouls was in session when Hank arrived. He took a seat outside and waited impatiently for his name to be called. He pitied the poor guy who was inside the courthouse; the Court weren't exactly renowned for their leniency.

Finally the trial was over, the sentencing carried out and Hank's name was called. He walked into the courtroom, trying to look confident. Everyone else in the room was sitting down but he was ordered to stay on his feet. The judge came into the room – the Court was now in session.

The judge was a scary looking guy. Well, he was a vampire after all. He was incredibly white and his black suit did nothing to help his pallor. He looked as though all his lifeblood had been sucked from him and his long bony fingers clutched the gavel. His eyes were small and beady, and his skin papery white. His skin was stretched tightly behind his ears and his ghostly smile revealed pointed, vampire-like teeth.

Hank looked at the jury. They were a motley crew, made up of creatures who had been rejected from other walks of un-dead life. They were thought unfit to carry out normal deathly duties so had been sent to the Court. Some of them took the form of animals and they squabbled and fought with one another continuously.

Hank felt his confidence begin to ebb away. There was no need for the case to be read out. The jury was aware of all the facts; they were merely there to give a verdict and for the judge to pass sentence. Hank fixed his eyes on the jury. The spokesperson got to his feet, clutching a piece of paper.

"Have you, the jury, reached a verdict?" he asked.

"We have, your honour," replied the spokesman.

The rest of the jurors sniggered, some pointing at Hank, others staring into space. They were now awaiting their next case, their interest in this one having waned. The piece of folded paper was passed to the judge and he opened it and read out one word:

"Guilty."

Hank shook his head. Well, well what a surprise. He had known the verdict before he had even entered the courtroom.

"So, what'd I do this time?" he asked, not really that interested. There was no point. He'd tried to protest his innocence before but once the Court of Ghouls had made their judgement, there seemed to be no going back.

The judge cleared his throat. "The function of the Grim Reaper," he began pompously, "is to monitor your progress, Mr Kane, is that correct?"

Hank nodded.

"Yet you called upon him for help when you should not have. You placed him in a situation where he felt he had no option *but* to help."

"Ah, come on," protested Hank. "He could have refused, couldn't he? Why does this always turn out to be my fault?"

The judge raised an eyebrow. "The Grim Reaper is not on trial here, Mr Kane. You are."

He brought down his gavel with a bang. "Case dismissed," he announced. "No need for me to repeat your sentence, Mr Kane. You will continue to solve crime on the streets of Glasgow but try and get it right this time."

Hank left the courtroom and walked outside. Annie and Charlie were waiting for him and looked at him expectantly.

"You're stuck with me for a little bit longer, kids," he said as they started to walk away from the court. "I'm not going to be allowed to pass over just yet!"

Behind Hank's back, Charlie and Annie smiled at one another. Though they wouldn't have admitted it to Hank, they would miss him when he finally went and were pleased he would be in Glasgow for a while longer.

Just then TG appeared at the steps of the court, moonlight glinting off his scythe.

"Need I ask how it went?"

"You know how it went. I swear TG, sometimes I wonder if you are really trying to help me pass over."

"Hank! How could you say such a thing?"

Charlie and Annie looked at each other and wondered why TG had jumped in to save them when Hank had it under control. And that was the reason the court gave for finding Hank guilty!

"C'mon," said TG, "let's go drown our sorrows at *The Cesspit*."

"Sounds too lovely to resist," said Hank, with a slight smile.

Was Glasgow growing on him, wondered Annie? Or did he just need a swig of his special potion!

# OTHER TITLES IN THE DEAD DETECTIVE SERIES:

## DEAD AND UNBURIED

Los Angeles 1953... and Private Detective Hank Kane doesn't know what's hit him. Lying face down on the same street he was just running down, he realises he's been shot. But instead of the morgue, Hank finds himself in the Court of Ghouls, in front of a Vampire judge and a jury of ghosts! He's on trial for cheating on his last case. His punishment? To get back to 'life' and solve a case honestly. Lippy 12-year-old Charlie Christian is assigned as his apprentice detective! The question is not, "will they solve the case?" but "will they solve it honestly?"

## SIX FEET UNDER

Hank falls and knocks himself out while chasing a thief from his office. He's forgotten to take his "medicine bottle" with him and his flesh starts disappearing, revealing his bony white skeleton underneath. Everybody is talking about the "well-dressed Skeleton" found lying in the street. His old-fashioned 1940s clothes and hat look very strange. The police, after forensic tests, have the body buried. Is this really the end of Hank Cane? It will be, unless Charlie can work out Hank's secret code in the letter in his desk drawer, marked "ONLY TO BE OPENED IN AN EMERGENCY". If this isn't an emergency what is? But can Charlie handle all the secrets in the letter?

### DEAD LOSS

Hank gets a visit from the ghost of murder victim Tony Falco, begging for help. Tony, a cat burglar, had stolen jewels on him when he died and the Court of Ghouls won't let Tony into Bandit Heaven until he returns them. Just one problem though – no-one found Falco's body. It's lost! Hank thinks that the Grim Reaper might have some clues. His apprentice, Charlie, is desperate to solve the case without help of any "dead guys", but he disappears! Now the Grim Reaper and Falco have a body full of loot to find – and the apprentice too!

## THE CORPSE THAT SANG

A Corpse seen in 1940's Los Angeles turns up in 2002, singing on TV! The strangest coincidence – or is Hank's old flame haunting him. She was a great detective who ended up in Sleuth Heaven – so, why give that up just to sing? Charlie sees the romantic side of Hank and wants to throw up! How can they solve cases with Hank staring at the TV all night? For the first time, Charlie has to take the calls at Hank's office. At last, the Kid can prove his worth, and he resolves to break the case of *The Corpse That Sang*.

## GHOST CAR 49

The siren from an old-fashioned American police car is heard echoing around the streets at night. The sound of screeching tyres, blaring police radio, 1940s jazz music and constant gunfire freak out the local residents. Needless to say, Charlie gets the call: "Better get over here, Kid. Looks like we've got something." But how will they bring Car 49 to a halt? And who is at the wheel?!

## THE DEAD DETECTIVE SERIES

www.booksnoir.com

www.deaddetective.com

---

*Hey guys! Hank Kane here. Check out my website* www.deaddetective.com *to keep up to date with my interactive e-book* Web of Intrigue, *an internet adventure where you, the reader, can help me on the case.*

*P.S. You'd better be good!*